Larry,
red and blue

by DIANE JARVIS JONES

When my best friend, Larry, was killed, my whole world fell apart. He had been a happy boy, a boy who wanted nothing more than to grow up and become a clown, and I was absolutely lost without him. I played by myself, but I wasn't really playing. I said little or nothing at all, and I preferred eating alone. I wouldn't sing, wouldn't share, wouldn't laugh. I was so quiet my dog didn't hear me when I opened the door, and nobody but nobody could make me smile.

I hated bedtime too because all my dreams had turned into nightmares. I sensed Larry was near but I couldn't see him, couldn't hear him, couldn't reach him. Most nights I'd wake up cold and frightened still clutching my teddy bear. Then I'd have to hide under the covers til morning. It was awful.

However, the very night I decided to grow up something magical happened. Without knowing it and while still sound asleep, I grabbed my crayon box, jumped back into my dream, and started chasing, chasing. And anything I caught I coloured.

Suddenly I was surrounded by cats and dogs and jelly beans, and kids with funny faces. When Larry appeared I threw down my crayons and ran to him. He smiled his Larry smile and held my hand while I told him how lonely I was, and how frightened I had become. He listened quietly, then said "Well, those days are over. You fought it out with your dreams tonight, Trixie, and you won. Big time. I'm proud of you, kid." He smiled and noogied my shoulder. "I told you I'd always be here for you. I meant it. So there." I grinned and noogied him back.

From then on I slept through the night.

In dreams I paint my Larry, my Larry, red and blue.
He talks to me and sings to me and loves me through and through.

Larry was seven when he died, and I had only turned five. Now I'm nine, but he'll always be seven. It's really weird. I still get goose bumps thinking about Larry, but its time to tell you the whole story anyway.

You see, I was only two when Larry moved onto our street. He was four. He didn't have to play with me, but he did. He shared everything with me: his trucks, his wagon, and his chips. He said I was the sister he never had. He said he liked my name, Emily, but he always called me Trixie.

Not everyone liked me, especially my brothers. They said I was a nuisance because I liked to bite, but I never bit Larry and Larry never bit me.

Unlike my brothers who ran from me, Larry wanted me to stay. He was patient and kind and could somehow ignore or explain all the disasters that followed me around. He laughed if I accidentally knocked over his building bricks or spilt milk on the floor. He wasn't mean and he didn't tease. And he didn't yell. Never. He liked me and he shared everything, including his magic buttons.

He sang to me and read to me and walked me round the house, him explaining this and that, and me licking up words like chocolate on a spoon.

I was just me full of giggles and spit.
And he was just he, full of stuff.
He was the magical prince in the book,
And I was the girl who played rough.

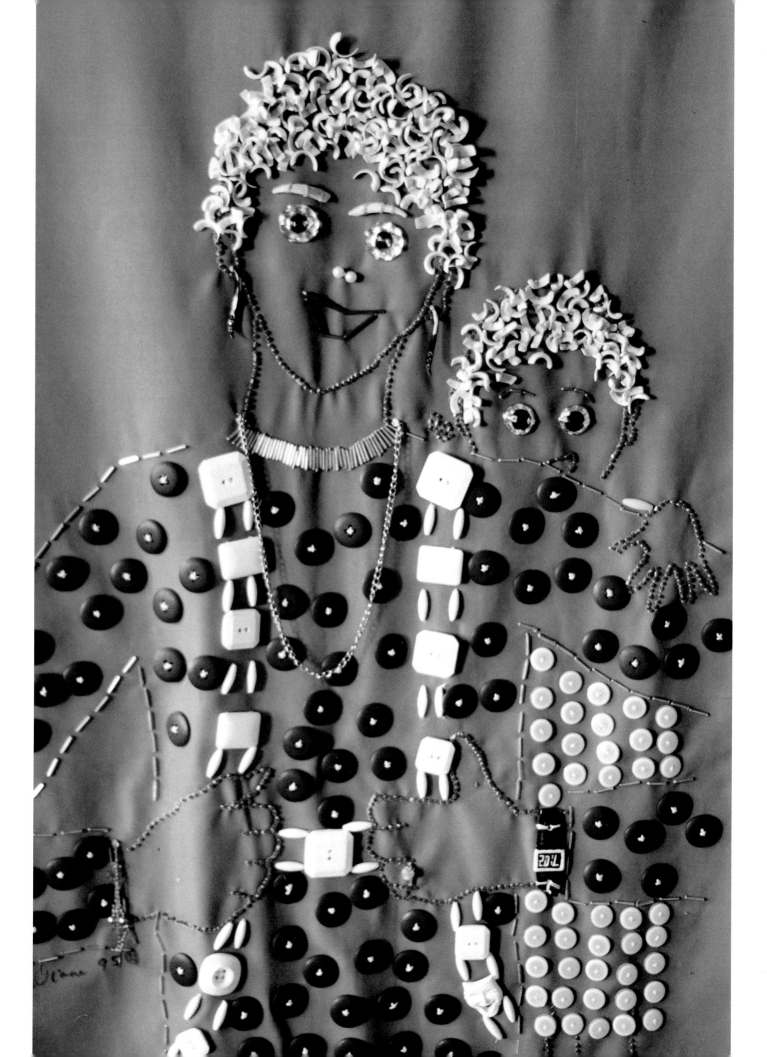

We grew as children grow and we knew what children know. We laughed and we played and wore socks made of sand.

> We loved to go on adventures.
> We loved to watch the sea.
> We loved the sand, the surf, the shells,
> and the man from Dickie Dee.
>
> We pushed the elevator buttons
> ignoring dirty looks.
> We were budding scientists.
> We were hunting crooks.
>
> Life was wonderful.

And then...

Up went down and left went right
and the rhythm fell flat as a cake.
Geese turned to pigs, and owls fled the night
and the elephant played with the snake.

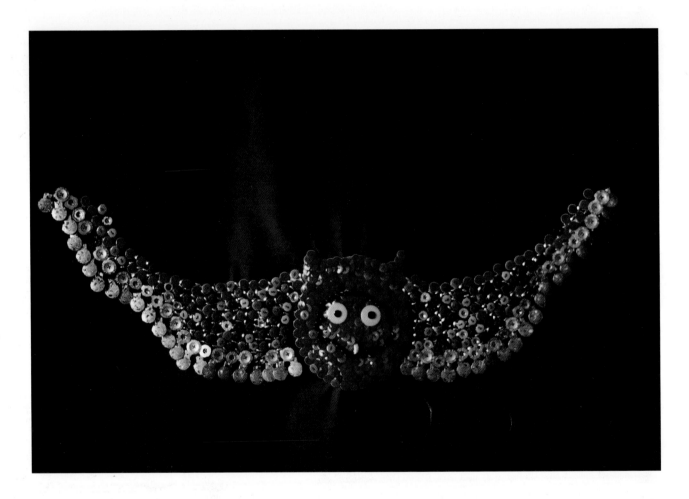

Caitlin Rose moved in next door. Ugh, how I hated that girl.

She was the same age as Larry and she was everything I wasn't. She was
a flowery girl, the sissy kind, the kind who could visit the Queen and never
spill tea. Her dolls never got dirty either, not like mine. She never had scabby
knees and she didn't like noise. Larry liked her, despite the fact that she didn't
like Miss Mildred McCreedy, his cat.

I wanted her gone, but Larry had other ideas. He adopted her the same way he adopted me. He said he knew something I didn't know, but he wouldn't tell me what it was.

Caitlin Rose was to stay. Caitlin Rose was to play. And that was that.

I really tried to like her. I really tried to care.
But I didn't like her squirmy legs, and I didn't like her hair.
I didn't like her little toe. I didn't like her nose.
I didn't like the way she scratched, and I didn't like her clothes.

She didn't like me either, not that she said so, but I knew what she was thinking.

She pretended to be as clever as Larry, and that really bugged me. She wasn't, of course. Nobody was as clever as he was. She was maybe half as clever, but that was all. She liked reading books and sometimes used big fancy words, words I didn't understand. Larry always made excuses for her, not that I cared. I did not like Caitlin Rose, and that's the truth.

Instead of going to sleep at night, I'd lie awake thinking up ways to scare her.

Big spider webs, huge spider webs,
gross spider webs would trap her.
With string strong enough, string thick enough,
string long enough to wrap her.

And there she would sit, and there she would lie,
and there she would pout, and there she would cry.

While I watched her feet being eaten.

Larry knew what I was thinking, all right. He told me so. Most times he'd roll his eyes,and mumble, "Trixxie," but once in a while he'd look hurt. "Has she been mean to you?" he'd ask. "Really mean?" I couldn't lieand say yes, even though I wanted to, so I said nothing. "She needs us,"he'd say. "My mom says her mom's got troubles right now, big troubles."

I pretended not to hear that. She seldom talked about home. She never complained, but we knew she was worried about something.

"You've seen her dog," he'd say. "Heard him whimpering. He's worried too, just like she is."

"No, she's not," I'd say. "She never said so."

"She doesn't have to," he'd answer. "We're her friends."

That made me roll my eyes.

No matter how often Caitlin Rose and I fought, Larry smoothed things over. But to me, play was never the same if Caitlin Rose was around. Christmas wasn't the same if Caitlin Rose was around. Ice cream didn't taste the same if Caitlin Rose was around. The only thing we didn't fight over were Larry's magic buttons. Those we strung, sorted, and shared.

Things got worse when they started grade one. I was still too young for kindergarten so was left behind all day. It was awful. On weekends I tried playing school with them but I wasn't very good at it. When new classmates started playing too, I really felt left out. Then they went into grade two and games got harder and harder. I could feel Caitlin Rose watching me, and I knew she was planning to do something.

After a horrible fight over popsicle sticks, Larry took me aside and said, "It's okay, Trixie. She's not that mad. She just thinks you're a bit of an enigma, that's all." As he walked away the word hit me. Enigma? Enigma! Caitlin Rose was calling me names.

I burst into tears. I had no idea what an enigma was, but I was sure it was mean and nasty. Sobbing, I blubbered out all the ways Caitlin Rose spoiled everything. I told him she was lying about having troubles at home, adding that I didn't care if she did. I reminded him that she took my dinosaur costume to school without asking for permission. And then I told him that I was never going to play with her again, and I ripped up my Button Bear card and threw it on the floor. I told him I hated her, hated her, hated her, and then I screamed, "I'm not an enigma! She is. And I wish she was dead."

And I slammed the door and ran home.

I was so upset I couldn't unclench my fists. When my brothers started teasing me I bit them both and was sent upstairs to my room. I was so upset I wouldn't talk to Mom or Dad. I fussed and I fumed and then I cried myself to sleep. It was such a sound sleep, I didn't hear the ambulance.

While I thrashed around in my bed, Larry was hit by a car and killed.
One minute he was riding his bike. The next he was lying on the road.
One minute he was waving to his mom. The next he was dead.
One minute he was my best friend. Then poof, he was gone.

I was stunned. Nothing had prepared me for this. Nothing. I never got a chance to say goodbye to him. I never got a chance to say I'm sorry. I never got another chance to be nice to him, to play, to smile, to share chips.

I cried and I cried because that was all I could do.

They said I was too young to go to the funeral. They said it might upset me. Couldn't they see I was upset already? Didn't they know I needed to be with Larry one more time? I told them I needed to see him. I told them I had things to say, but they wouldn't listen. Why?

I never got a chance to say goodbye to him, or to say I'm sorry. I never got another chance to be nice, to play, to smile, to share chips.

And that's when my dreams turned scary.

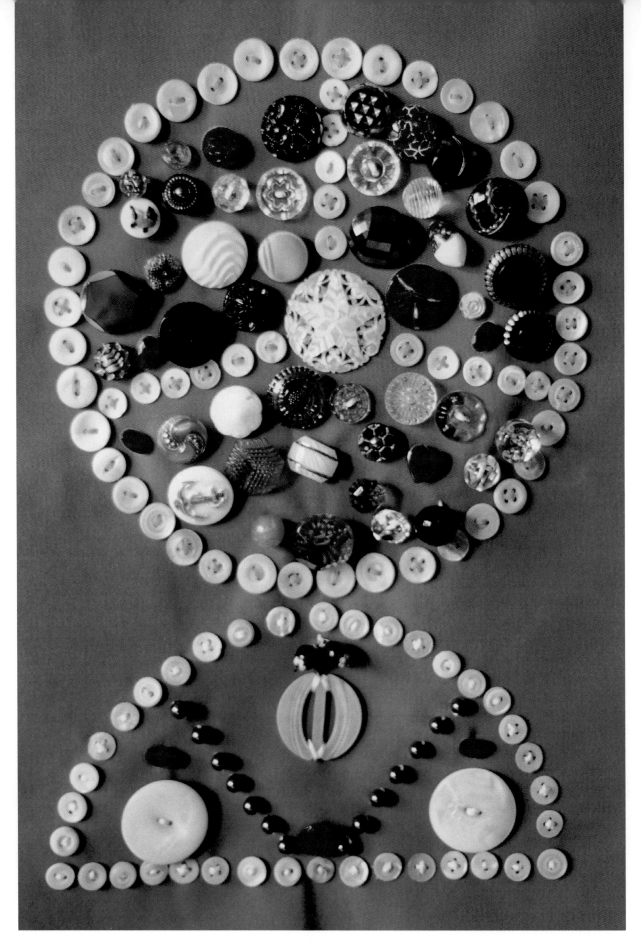

Each day brought new troubles. A sign said Larry's house was for sale.
People came. People went. Some smiled. Some didn't. Some looked up. Some
looked down. One man fell down the steps. Nobody bought Larry's house.

Birthdays didn't interest me. Mine came and went and I didn't even eat my cake. Grade one began, not that I cared. My feet took me to parties but I didn't have any fun. School was hard for me, very hard. Even the pictures I drew looked stupid. My smiles were hidden so deep in my pockets, they just wouldn't fall out.

I blamed myself for Larry's death, but was afraid to tell anyone. I knew everyone, including my mom, would hate me for having been so mean. Being alone all the time made me feel smaller and smaller while things that frightened me got bigger. Kids at school started saying I was weird and they pushed their desks away from mine. Then at recess they'd whisper things and giggle. It was awful.

Caitlin Rose did come to visit but I wouldn't play with her.

My mother told my brothers to be nicer to me and they did try, but the stories they read to me always sounded strange. Games weren't much fun either. Once just for fun I bit them both, and the old grins lit up our faces. We noogied and teased, but the fun didn't last. I never knew a heart could feel so broken.

The months dragged on and on and on. The odd day was fun, but most were sad, and all were terribly lonely. In time I did stop throwing things. But when the nightmares got too bad, I sometimes wet the bed. My brothers teased me about that, and about sucking my thumb, but I didn't care. It was my thumb and I was sad, so there.

After school I sat with my fish. Larry had once said that they blew kisses at people with sad little eyes, at people who looked like me. And he was right.

In early October Caitlin Rose came to my door. We stared at each other, neither one saying a word. I had learned that enigma meant being mysterious, or puzzling, and full of wonderful surprises. It wasn't a nasty word at all. It was a good word, a fine word, a word that children need to know. I realized that Caitlin Rose was just as smart as Larry.

Larry had been right. She was as mysterious to me as I was to her. Being an enigma was good, I decided, and secretly I was proud to be one. Still, I said nothing.

"Larry's house has been sold," she said. "New people will be moving in soon. Come Emily," and she pulled me outside.

This time I followed. Even in the sunshine Larry's house looked bruised and hurt. We crawled up the steps. Soon my fingers started peeling paint and I was overcome with sadness. The cold October wind whipped up our hair and we huddled together like two old ladies, saying nothing.

Caitlin Rose came for me every day and every day we huddled a little closer. One day our fingers touched. Only then did we speak.

I burst into tears and told her I never got a chance to say goodbye to Larry, or to say I was sorry for all the trouble I had caused. I told her I was sad because I would never get another chance to be nice to him, to smile, to play, or to share chips. And she listened to my every word.

When I finished she whispered, "You know Emily, I never got a chance to say goodbye to him either. He was my best friend too, and I miss him as much as you do." It was my turn to listen to her every word. She pulled out the magic button egg that Larry had made for her, and handed it to me. Larry made button eggs for everyone. Mine was lost. I held her egg, loved it, and kissed it twice. Then I handed it back to her, and she smiled. That's when I knew we were becoming friends.

With Caitlin Rose, I could talk and cry.
I no longer had to fight her.
With Caitlin Rose, I could be me,
And I no longer wanted to bite her.

I was no longer alone. Kids at school noticed my smiles again, real smiles, big smiles, and they started smiling back at me. Somehow the words in books got easier to read and nine and fourteen added up to twenty-three, not just once in a while, but each and every time.

Caitlin Rose loves playing the piano. Last week, just for fun, we sang Happy Birthday three times, once for Larry, once for her, and once for me. It was the first time I'd sung since Larry's death, and it felt wonderful.

I discovered I really liked her. I discovered I really cared.
I really liked her squirmy legs and I really liked her hair.
I began to like her little toe, and I began to like her nose.
And I loved the way she laughed and scratched, and I loved her pretty clothes.

She asked if she could call me Trixie, and I said yes. Then she helped me make a new Halloween costume and I finally won a prize. That was the night I brought crayons into my dream. That was the night I found Larry.

Caitlin Rose and I don't have a perfect friendship, not like the one I had with Larry. There are still some things we don't like about each other, just as there are many things that we do. Even so, we are loyal as puppies. We are sorry we fought so much back then. We learned our lesson and now let some words go unsaid.

No matter what, Larry is never far from our thoughts. Just thinking about him reminds us to laugh and to share. To honour him we started up his old Button Bear Club, gave out cards, and taught our new members, Julie, May Ling and Sam all the secrets of playing and making things with buttons.

Sometimes Caitlin Rose and I run off and have a Larry day, a day just for us. Sometimes it's sad. Sometimes it's not. We know how hard it is to lose a best friend so we're careful with each other. After a Larry day we always feel comfortable, like a string of pearls.

This year we bottled buttons and tossed them out to sea. Caitlin Rose enclosed a note about Larry and I drew a picture of a button egg. Caitlin Rose thinks I'm a little silly, but I know some day whales will swim beside our buttons. And I know in my heart of hearts, children who live far far away, children with names like Etsu, Maya, and Carlos, will some day scoop our buttons from the sea, and think about making a button egg.

In dreams I play with Larry, my Larry, red and blue.
He talks to me and sings to me and loves me through and through.
Each day he goes collecting, his buttons from the skies,
And each night he puts thc bluest ones deep inside my eyes.
He'll always be my best friend, so there's no need to cry.
He wants to stay, he wants to play, we'll never say goodbye.

Caitlin Rose is my new best friend, for always and always, and more.
She makes me laugh. She makes me run. She's waiting at the door.
Our words are soft. Our thoughts are kind. We don't want to make a slip,
for we've learned to smile, and we've learned to play, and we've learned to
share our chips.

Diane Jarvis Jones, author, artist, and publisher, is also a teacher and cab driver who lives in Vancouver, Canada. In kindergarten she wore a Little Red Riding Hood costume to her first Halloween party and won a prize: a pen. She thought pens were silly gifts for children who couldn't write, yet she warmed it with her hands and loved it. Many years would pass before she discovered that in addition to teaching, she was meant to write stories that give hope to children who have suffered a great loss.

Diane Jarvis Jones' Button Books, for children of all ages, are written in a child's voice. They describe the shock and the sadness that accompany death. Grief is honestly and sensitively portrayed, yet children are always left with meaningful legacies.

AUNT MARY BUTTONS discusses the terminal illness of a beloved aunt. The first book in the series, it has been recommended by the BC Ministry of Education for school libraries. The book has been reviewed and recommended by hospices, agencies concerned with AIDS, ALS, cancer, and by child advocacy groups.

LARRY, red and blue describes the accidental death of a best friend. Nine year old Trixie describes the friendship, the shock of death, the loneliness, the troubles at school, and finally healing and the acceptance of new friends.

The button banners, all original artwork, were created and hand sewn for each story. A labour of love, they take months to sew before Diane can photograph them. Made with buttons and recycled jewelry and junk, they range in size from 55 x150cm to 150 x150cm. Always on display at author readings, they delight adults and children alike. The banners have been exhibited in western Canada.